TOO YOUNG

SALLY WONG

Illustrated by
Elif Balta Parks

To My Beloved Husband, you are my Love and support.

To my children, you are the Light of my Life, and you make a difference to me every day.

On the way home from school, Niren told Mikki about a girl who saved a baby from a fire.

"Wow!" exclaimed Mikki. "I wish that we could be heroes!"

"Me too," agreed Niren. "I hope a fire like that doesn't happen to us, but maybe we can just try to be helpful in little ways."

The two children sat on the porch. Looking
out for anyone who needed their help.

They saw their neighbour. Mrs. Lee. standing
on a ladder by her house.

"Hi Mrs. Lee! Do you need some help?" Niren asked.

"Hmm." Mrs. Lee said. Looking around. "There's nothing here for you two because you're too young."

"Too young?" asked Mikki.

"Oh, I just mean there's only dangerous jobs to do here." Mrs. Lee smiled. "But thank you for your offer."

7

Niren and Mikki sighed as they walked down the sidewalk.

8

They saw Mr. Jelani in his garden.
He was mowing the very tall grass.

"Ooooo, Mr. Jelani's really old and needs lots of help!" Mikki cried.

As they raced over to him, Niren exclaimed, "Do you need help, Mr. Jelani?"

"Oh that's so nice of you." Mr. Jelani replied. "But you're a bit too young to help with this chore."

"Too young?" Mikki pouted.

"Lawnmowers can be dangerous. I don't want you to get hurt."

11

Niren and Mikki shrugged and kept walking, kicking rocks as they went.

"Why won't anyone let us help?" Niren blurted.

"Everyone thinks we're too young to help," Mikki said, looking down at her shoes.

"Maybe Mrs. Sato will let us help her," Niren said.

They walked over to Mrs. Sato's house.
She was carrying something that
Looked Like a big pair of scissors.

Mrs. Sato, those scissors look heavy!"
Mikki called out.

"Oh, they're not scissors." Mrs. Sato replied.
"They're pruning shears for the garden."

"Do you need help carrying them?" Niren asked.

"Thank you for offering." Mrs. Sato said, smiling. "But you're too young to handle pruning shears."

16

"Too young? But why?" Mikki asked.

"The blades are very sharp." Mrs. Sato answered. "It's too dangerous for you."

Mikki nodded, shoving her hands in her pockets as she and Niren started walking back home.

"Maybe we really are too young to help people," Mikki grumbled, sulking as she walked.

They continued their walk back on the dusty sidewalk, with their hands in their pockets.

19

When they got home, Niren slammed the door behind them and plopped onto the floor. "We can't do *anything* to help!" He crossed his arms.

"There must be something we can do," Mikki said.

"You got any ideas?" Niren asked.

"Nah. I got nothin'," Mikki replied.

Behind them, their mother rushed around, slamming pots on the stove and wiping up a spill on the floor. The phone rang and rang and their baby brother, Jin, ran around the house naked and screaming.

21

"What is all the noise about?"
Niren yelled. turning his head.

"It's hard to think when there's
such a racket!" added Mikki.

"Hey kids!" Mom called. "I could use a little help!"

Mikki and Niren turned and looked at their mother. She was leaning on the counter with her hair frazzled, tomato sauce on her blouse, and an exhausted look on her face.

Suddenly. Niren and Mikki's eyes went wide.

"Mom! I can help you with Jin!" Niren announced.

"And I can help put the dishes away!" Mikki declared.

25

Mom stared in awe as Niren and Mikki buzzed around the house, taking care of the chores. Niren changed Jin into a brand-new diaper and wiped the dirt off his face while Mikki cleaned all the dishes.

When they finished, Niren and Mikki smiled so big, they could count each other's teeth!

Mom chuckled and gave them a big, wet kiss. "Thank you, Niren and Mikki," she said.

"You're welcome, Mom!" They giggled as they squeezed their mom in a hug.

Just then, their Dad walked in with an empty garbage can in his hands.

"Dad!" Niren called. "Can we help you pick up garbage?"

Without giving Dad a chance to answer, Mikki snatched the trash can out of his hands. Both kids ran around the house and filled the can with garbage. Their dad scratched his head and chuckled.

"We aren't too young to help with the trash, Dad!" Niren said.

"Yeah, it's not too dangerous for us!" Mikki giggled.

"Thank you, guys!" Dad laughed.

Later that night, Niren and Mikki stayed up late, making a list of little things they could do to help out around the house.

"I can dust, make my bed and read stories to Jin." Niren decided.

"And I can sweep the walkway and water the grass." Mikki said.

"What are you two doing up so late?" Mom asked, opening the bedroom door.

"And what are you talking about?" Dad added.

Mikki smiled. "We're talking about how to help around the house."

"Well in that case," Dad replied, "Stay up as late as you want!"

Mom smiled. "You are both growing up so fast."

Mikki shook her head. "Nah, we're still young."

"Just not *too* young!" Niren added.

Laughing, they got into bed, made a few more plans, and then fell fast asleep.

Tips for Parents/Guardians

Hi Parents, you are the cornerstone of kids making a difference in this world. Sometimes kids want to become superheroes who swoop in to save the day. What they need to know is that they need to start small and make a difference in the lives of people who are closest to them, like their family. What can we do to help foster kids' desires to help others? Here are a few ideas parents have shared.

Helping with the dishes (without breaking any plates!): Get a plastic washbasin. Fill it with water and some dishwashing liquid. If necessary, place the washbasin on a chair for easy access. Then they can wash the unbreakable cups and dishes.

Taking out the Garbage (and avoid the big mess!): Place less messy garbage (e.g., unsoiled wraps, cups, plastic items) in a separate bag. Get kids to grab as many bags as they can and put them in a suitable garbage bin.

Danger-Free Cooking: Ask kids to help wash vegetables and fruits in a bin. With very close monitoring, allow them to stir batter and pour things that are a suitable size. My children love to eat, so they are often willing to help in the kitchen.

Household Cleaning: Ask kids to sweep the floor or dust shelves and tables. Get a broom that is kid-sized and ask them to sweep. Remove breakables and valuables to avoid damage.

Visit with Grandma and Grandpa: Give your kids flowers from the garden and ask them to bring the flowers when you go to visit. You can even let the kids decorate the bunch of flowers with twine, ribbons, etc. Grandparents love to see their grandchildren embracing their talents. Encourage your kids to share their natural gifts with their grandparents, or encourage your kids to play a fun game with them.

Adopt a Park: Once a week/month, bring your kids to the park. Bring gloves and a garbage bag. Clear the park of any litter.

We would love to hear more ideas about what parents are doing to help their kids to make a difference! Send us your ideas and/or pictures to: **sallywongstudios@gmail.com.**

About the Author

Sally Wong grew up in the bustling city of Toronto. She is an elementary school teacher and has been working with children for many years. *Too Young* Is her first published book. She wrote *Too Young* 15 years ago, after she was inspired by the kids around her who made a positive difference in her Life. She Lives with her husband, 3 kids, and Bernadoodle. Sally Loves the great Canadian Landscape and is inspired by the music around her. She would like to do more humanitarian work and also wants to be a hero, just Like Niren and Mikki.

You can connect with Sally on her website at www.sallywongstudios.ca.

About the Illustrator

Elif Balta Parks is a cheese Lover, hamster-admirer, chocolate connoisseur and a prolific children's book illustrator. She grew up in Istanbul, Turkey, next to the bright and blue Bosporus. Even as a child she knew she wanted to be an artist. She has completed a degree in Business and went on to study at Central St. Martins School of Fine Art for a short time before beginning to work on her first children's books.

Elif strives for bright and cheerful illustrations that capture the joy of childhood. Since starting her professional career, she has illustrated many books (all she needs is a warm chair, some tea and a cat around). Elif currently Lives in Shropshire with her husband, their cat and Dean Martin, who is always singing from the stereo while she works.

32

Manufactured by Amazon.ca
Bolton, ON